A CAPTAIN CRITTER READER

WELLINGTON PELICAN

Story and pictures by Bob Reese

ARO Publishing

MY 35 WORDS ARE:

Wellington	short	all
Pelican	skinny	'those
he	legs	things
is	big	you
a	feet	say
funny	little	I
sort	head	am
long	beak	think
in	eyes	we
the	wins	are
front	looks	all
back	with	

Library of Congress Cataloging in Publication Data
Reese, Bob.
   Wellington Pelican: story and pictures.
   (Captain Critter Reader)
   Summary: Describes Wellington Pelican, a bird who
does not sing but just sits.
   [1.   Pelicans – Fiction.   2.   Stories in rhyme]
I.   Title.   II.   Series.
ISBN 0-89868-572-9 – Library Bound
ISBN 0-89868-573-7 – Soft Bound

funny sort.

He is long

in the front.

In the back

he is short.

Skinny legs.

Big feet.

Little head.
Big beak.

15

Little eyes.

Big wings.

He looks funny

with all those things!"

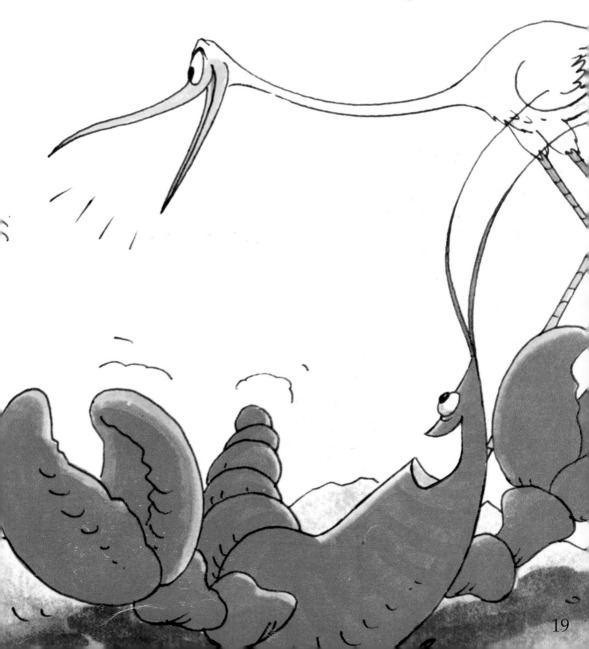

"You say I am big,

little, long, short.

I think we are all
a funny sort!"

Bob Reese

Story teller, writer and artist, Bob Reese has written and illustrated over 100 books for beginning readers.

Bob Reese was born in 1938 in Hollywood, California. His mother Isabelle was an English teacher in the Los Angeles city Schools.

After his graduation from high school he went to work for Walt Disney Studios as an animation cartoonist. He received his B.S. degree in Art and Business and began work as a freelance illustrator and designer.